If
you'd like to see Frumpy grow
send
an E-Mail to those you know

The Frumpy McDoogle series for girls and boys

DESTINED TO BE A CLASSIC!

FRUMPY McDOOGLE
And The Legend
of the
Ruby Toad

Story by Frever Fields
Pictures by Jennifer Camillo
Frumpy's Portrait by Anna Anderson

KimberLite
Publishing
Co.
www.frumpybooks.com

Other books in the Frumpy McDoogle Series

Current Books

1. Frumpy McDoogle:
   The Boy Who Made a Poem
2. Frumpy McDoogle:
   And the Legend of the Ruby Toad

Future Books

3. Frumpy McDoogle:
   And The Cave of the Williwaw Wind
4. Frumpy McDoogle:
   Meets The Elf King of Buttonwillow
5. Frumpy McDoogle:
   Meets The Boy From The Hassayampa

6. Frumpy McDoogle:
   And The Treasure of Palaka Madro

7. Frumpy McDoogle:
   Meets The Giant From Wapompa

8. Frumpy McDoogle:
   And a Cow Named Betsy

9. Frumpy McDoogle:
   And The Ghost on Walker's Spit

10. Frumpy McDoogle:
    And a Dog Named Skunkwhiskers

www.frumpybooks.com

Frumpy McDoogle: And the Legend of the Ruby Toad
© 2003 By Frever Fields
All Rights Reserved
No portion of this book may be reproduced in any manner without the
written permission of the publisher, Kimberlite Publishing Co.
44091 Olive Avenue, Hemet, California 92544-2609 — (909) 927-7726
Printed in China

ISBN 0-9632675-1-5

Frumpy McDoogle: And the Legend of the Ruby Toad
By Frever Fields; Illustrated by Jennifer Camillo

Edited by Melissa Montgomery
Photo (back cover) by Erik Melgaard

Summary: A boy with a problem turns to his best friend, Poogle,
the littlest elf of all, who holds the perfect solution.

First printing August, 2003

This book is dedicated to our Creator and to dreamers everywhere; to Eric Weber for his expertise in publishing; to my wife, Tonnie, the beacon who stays me from the rocks, the tether that pulls me down from the clouds; to Ransom Hess for all his work; to my illustrator, Jennifer Camillo, whose pictures give life to the stories; to my editor, Melissa Montgomery, and her razor sharp pencil; and to all my beloved readers, whose love and encouragement helped to launch the Frumpy McDoogle Series.

Frever Fields

LET YOUR HEART ROAM THROUGH THE FIELDS

FREVER FIELDS

rumpy had a problem, a big problem. His father, who worked as a lumberjack, got hurt in the woods and could no longer do his job. What little savings the family had was quickly being used up to pay bills and put food on the table. Soon they would have no money left to pay the man from whom they had bought their cozy little house, the house Frumpy was born in, the only house he had ever known.

In the weeks after his father's accident, Frumpy did everything he could think of to earn money to help pay the bills. He borrowed his mother's cast-iron skillet to pan for gold in the little creek that ran behind their house, but he never found even a speck of gold.

He collected bottles and newspapers, but he only earned a few dollars at best. Unless he could think of some way to make more money, the family was in danger of losing the very roof over their heads.

rumpy was beside himself; then, Poogle popped into his mind. "That's it!" Frumpy said. "That's it! I'll just ask Poogle what to do!"

Poogle, the elf, was Frumpy's very best friend in all the world. He was the littlest elf of all—but the smartest person Frumpy ever met. Poogle knew the answer to just about everything.

"Now," Frumpy thought, "where in all elfdom should I go to find my little friend?" Then Frumpy remembered the huckleberries. Poogle loved huckleberries, and he knew the very best place to get them—the huckleberriest huckleberry patch there ever was!

The next morning, Frumpy set out to find Poogle; and just as he had thought, he found him smack dab in the middle of a patch, shoving huckleberries down his tiny throat as fast as he could pick them. Poogle looked up and noticed the worried look on Frumpy's face and said, "Let's go down by the stream. I'll wash off this berry juice, and then we can sit and talk."

Frumpy told Poogle the whole sad tale; then, he asked if Poogle knew how they could make some money. Poogle put his tiny hand on Frumpy's arm. Then, looking up with a big smile on his face, he said, "I sure do!"

Frumpy said, "How? Tell me how?"

It was then, while sitting in the dreamy sunshine on the bank of the stream, that Poogle began telling Frumpy *The Legend of the Ruby Toad.*

"It all happened a long time ago, many years before you were even born. A wicked wizard lived in a castle on the mountain called 'Crooked Peak.' The wizard had a twisted sense of humor, and he used his magic to play awful tricks on the farmers and village people."

Frumpy asked, "What kind of tricks?"

"Well," Poogle said, "once he made all the corn pop, right in the fields! It looked like a snowstorm had hit—right in the middle of summer! It was so deep it covered a whole wagon—horses too!"

Frumpy asked, "Couldn't the farmers have sold the popcorn?"

Poogle said, "Maybe, but the wizard made a big wind come up, and it all blew away before they could save it!"

oogle went on to tell Frumpy that, another time, the wizard turned all the cows' milk into fruit juice. There was grape, orange, and strawberry.

"Well," Frumpy said, "people like fruit juice."

Poogle laughed, "Yes, but with no milk, the people couldn't make any cream, butter, or cheese. Then one day, the wizard did something even worse! He made the wheels on everything turn into squares. This made things so bumpy that kids couldn't ride their tricycles or bicycles, mothers couldn't push their baby strollers, hay fell off the wagons, and all the wheelbarrows went bumpity, bumpity, bump!

The people had reached their breaking point. They had to find a way to get rid of this wizard. Someone had an idea. They could ask the hideous looking dragon, who lives in the Valley of the Long Shadows, if he would scare the wizard away. 'But,' they wondered, 'what can we give the dragon for coming to our aid?'

Then a man named Goody Gotfreed told everyone that the ground where the dragon lives is almost solid rock, so no apple trees can grow there. And, he remembered hearing, the dragon's favorite food in all the world is apple pie. He would do anything for apple pie!

hat made this dragon sooooo ugly was bumps, lumps and lumps of icky, pewy bumps, and each bump oozed a sulfurous liquid that smelled like rotten eggs; however, the dragon could turn this liquid into fire and breathe it out his nose!

That same day, the people went to see the dragon; and as luck would have it, they made a deal: the dragon would chase the wizard away – for five hundred and five apple pies.

The very next morning, everyone stayed home from work to bake apple pies. There were pies, pies, and more pies. They were cooling on windowsills, sitting on porch steps, and even tottering atop fence posts.

People were loading them into baby buggies, wheelbarrows, and wagons; and more were baking in the ovens. Even the air smelled like apple pie. They baked and worked and worked and baked until they finally reached the magic number—five hundred and five apple pies.

Then they waited, tingling with excitement because of what was about to happen. First they felt the ground begin to shake, then they heard this terrible roar, and then they smelled the biggest stink that ever stunk! It was happening! It was real! The dragon had come to scare the wizard away!

The dragon then began to climb the mountain, each step going Boom! Boom! Boom! First he tried to stink the wizard out, then he roared his roarriest roar, and then, he breathed fire into the windows! That scared the wizard so much that he took his wife and ran.

Howard, the next day, the wizard sent a note to the village saying he wanted to talk to all of the people one more time before he left for good. The note said for everyone to go to the giant tree stump just outside the village where the wizard would be waiting.

So everyone went to see the wizard. When they arrived, he was standing on top of the stump.

'First,' he said, 'I would like to apologize for all the mean things I have done to you. And to prove that I am sorry, I have decided to give you a great and wonderful gift, a gift that will bring you laughter, happiness, and prosperity for many years to come.'

The wizard then raised his wand, and everyone held their breath to see what would happen. Then he said these magic words:

> 'Ooktus, pooktus, catus, zoad,
> Create for me a big green toad.
> And in his mouth, a brilliant jewel,
> That he will keep from every fool.
> Who makes him laugh shall have in hand
> The greatest ruby in the land!'

There was a big puff of smoke, and when it cleared, sitting on the ground was a toad, the biggest—and greenest!—toad anyone had ever seen, and in his mouth was a sparkling ruby!

hen the wizard went on to explain: 'The only way the ruby can be taken from the toad's mouth is to make him laugh. But here's the rub. The toad has almost no sense of humor.

The first part of your gift will come when you laugh yourselves silly telling your funniest jokes and stories to the toad. That will make you happy.

As the legend spreads, people will come from miles away and then from the far corners of the world seeking to capture the ruby with new jokes and stories that will make you laugh. And all these people will pay you money for food, clothing, and shelter, and so you shall prosper.'

The wizard then said three magic words, the ground shook, and he disappeared with his wife, forever!"

After hearing the legend, Frumpy really wanted that ruby. "But," he asked, "if no one has ever made the toad laugh, how can we?"

Poogle said not to worry. He had a plan.

"But where does the toad live?" Frumpy asked.

"In a cave," said Poogle, "near the base of Thunder Mountain. But being older now, he spends most of his days sleeping and only comes out at night."

Poogle continued. "Now, I'll make a list of things for you to get from the village."

Poogle took a twig, dipped it in some berry juice, and wrote the list on a piece of white bark. There were nine things on the list: a long black wig, a red scarf, a powder puff, a black top hat, a cigar, a pair of horn-rimmed glasses, some red lipstick, a hand mirror, and a chicken feather.

Poogle said, "Collect all these things, put them in a pillowcase, and meet me at the base of Thunder Mountain."

It took Frumpy several days to fill the list. Then he met Poogle, who had already found the cave hidden among some pucker bushes. As they got closer and closer to the entrance, they could hear the toad snoring loudly. Then they tip-toed in and went to work.

Very softly (and very quietly), they put the long black wig on top of the toad's head. Then they powdered his face until he was white as a ghost. They smeared the red lipstick on his lips, perched the black top hat on his head, set the horn-rimmed glasses on his nose, put the red scarf around his neck, and stuck the cigar in his mouth.

Then, Poogle told Frumpy to hold the mirror right in front of the toad, and Poogle tickled the toad with the feather. The toad began to squirm, and Poogle tickled him some more. One eye opened a crack; then both eyes popped open. At first, the toad didn't know where he was; but as his eyes cleared, he saw in the mirror the most ridiculous looking toad there ever was—and didn't even know it was himself!

His belly started to shake; his lips began to quiver; and just as his mouth started to open, Frumpy grabbed the ruby. The mouth opened wider-and wider! And then, the deepest, loudest, richest, laughiest laugh that was ever laughed blasted out of the cave and even shook the pucker bushes.

Frumpy and Poogle danced around, holding the ruby high in the air. Then they skipped outside and started jumping up and down, shouting at the tops of their voices, "We did it! We did it! We made the toad laugh!"

Next Book in the Frumpy Series

FRUMPY McDOOGLE And The Cave of the Williwaw Wind

KimberLite Publishing Co.

www.frumpybooks.com

If
you'd like to see Frumpy grow
send
an E-Mail to those you know

The Frumpy McDoogle series for girls and boys

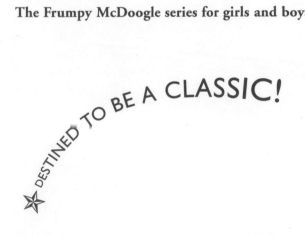

DESTINED TO BE A CLASSIC!